For

Mimi Kayden

First published 1996 in Great Britain by
Walker Books Ltd
87 Vauxhall Walk
London SE11 5HJ

First published 1995 by
Dial Books for Young Readers, New York

Text © 1996 Rosemary Wells
Illustrations © 1995 Rosemary Wells

This book has been typeset in Cochin.

Printed in Hong Kong

British Library Cataloguing in Publication Data
A catalogue record for this book is
available from the British Library.

ISBN 0-7445-4488-2

EDWARD'S
FIRST SWIMMING PARTY

ROSEMARY WELLS

WALKER BOOKS
AND SUBSIDIARIES
LONDON • BOSTON • SYDNEY

"Edward," asked Edward's mum,
"are you ready for Georgina's
birthday party?"

"The party's at the swimming pool,"
said Edward's dad.
"Let's get your swimming trunks."

"We'll wrap Georgina's present
in the prettiest paper," said
Edward's mum.

"Are you sure you want to wear those water wings?" asked Edward's mum.

"You swam last summer without
water wings," Edward's
dad reminded him.

But Edward would not take
off his water wings.

Georgina's mother welcomed
Edward to the party.

Everybody sang,
"Happy birthday, Georgina!"

Edward was the only one
wearing water wings.

He heard Georgina whisper
to her best friend, Ivy,
"Only sissies wear water wings!"

But Edward didn't care
what Georgina said.

"He's so sweet, let's give
him a great big hug!" whispered
Georgina to Ivy.

Georgina and Ivy hugged
Edward so tight that they popped
his water wings.

"Oops!" they said.

But Edward floated nicely.
Georgina was in big trouble.

Then everyone sang, "Happy birthday to Edward!" three times.

The lifeguard called Edward's
mum and dad.

"He's just not ready for this kind of party," said the lifeguard.

"Not everyone is ready for the
same things at the same time," said
Edward's mum and dad.

On the way home Edward
asked for new water wings …

just in case!

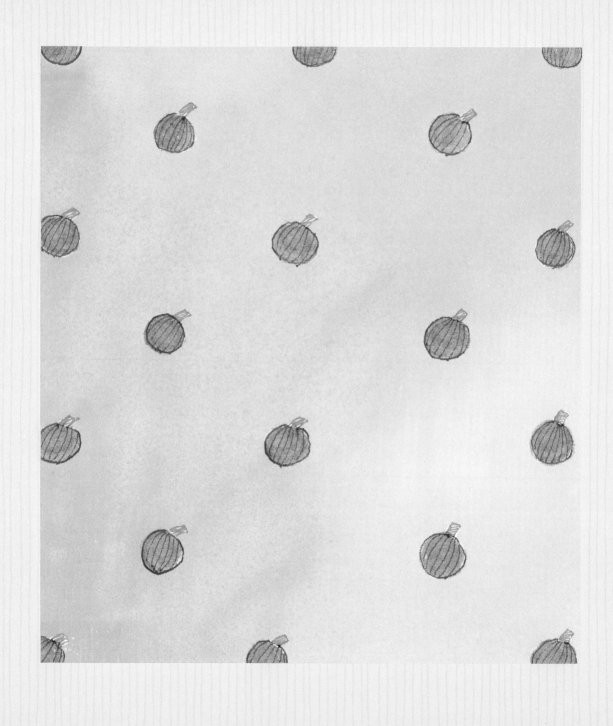